Put Beginning Readers on the Right Track with
ALL ABOARD READING™

The All Aboard Reading series is especially for beginning readers. Written by noted authors and illustrated in full color, these are books that children really and truly *want* to read—books to excite their imagination, tickle their funny bone, expand their interests, and support their feelings. With four different reading levels, All Aboard Reading lets you choose which books are most appropriate for your children and their growing abilities.

Picture Readers—for Ages 3 to 6
Picture Readers have super-simple texts, with many nouns appearing as rebus pictures. At the end of each book are 24 flash cards—on one side is the rebus picture; on the other side is the written-out word.

Level 1—for Preschool through First-Grade Children
Level 1 books have very few lines per page, very large type, easy words, lots of repetition, and pictures with visual "cues" to help children figure out the words on the page.

Level 2—for First-Grade to Third-Grade Children
Level 2 books are printed in slightly smaller type than Level 1 books. The stories are more complex, but there is still lots of repetition in the text, and many pictures. The sentences are quite simple and are broken up into short lines to make reading easier.

Level 3—for Second-Grade through Third-Grade Children
Level 3 books have considerably longer texts, harder words, and more complicated sentences.

All Aboard for happy reading!

Library of Congress Cataloging-in-Publication Data

Mason, Jane B.
  The flying horse: the story of Pegasus / by Jane B. Mason; illustrated by Susan Swan
    p. cm. — (All aboard reading)
  Summary: With the help of the goddess Athena, a young prince tames the winged horse
Pegasus and destroys a dreaded monster.
  1. Pegasus (Greek mythology) — Juvenile literature. [1. Pegasus (Greek mythology)
2. Mythology, Greek.] I. Swan, Susan Elizabeth, ill. II. Title. III. Series.
BL820.P4M37 1999
398.2 0938 0454—dc21   98-53367
                                                                                  CIP
ISBN 0-448-42051-1 (GB) A B C D E F G H I J   AC
ISBN 0-448-41980-7(pbk) A B C D E F G H I J

**ALL
ABOARD
READING™**

Level 1
Preschool-Grade 1

The Flying Horse

The Story of Pegasus

**By Jane B. Mason
Illustrated by Susan Swan**

Grosset & Dunlap • New York

Long, long ago, there was
a horse named Pegasus.
(You say it like this: PEG-a-sis.)
Pegasus had a long white mane
and a long white tail.

On his back were two wings.
Pegasus was a magic horse.
He could fly!

Pegasus lived on a mountain
near the home of the gods.
Pegasus played with
the children of the gods.
He gave them rides
across the sky.

One day a goddess
came to see Pegasus.
Her name was Athena.
(You say it like this:
uh-THEE-na.)
"It is time for you
to leave here,"
she said.
"It is time for you
to do great things."

Athena rode
Pegasus down to a lake.
There, fast asleep,
was a young prince.

Athena said,

"There is a terrible beast.

It has killed many people.

It has set fire

to many homes.

The prince must kill

the beast.

He needs your help."

Then Athena gave the prince
a dream.
In the dream the prince
had a magic spear.
He rode a magic horse.

Soon the prince woke up.
Next to him was a spear,
just like the spear
in his dream.
What else did he see?

A white horse with wings,
just like the horse
in the dream.
Pegasus stomped his feet
and shook his head.
He trotted over to
the prince.
He nuzzled the prince
with his nose.

The prince climbed on
the horse.
Off they flew.
The prince was on his
way to find the beast!

From up in the sky
the prince saw a cave.
Curls of smoke—
strange green smoke—
came out of the cave.
This was the home of the beast!

The prince and Pegasus
landed near the cave.
Piles of bones were
on the ground.
They were bones of
animals and people.

Then a roar came
from the cave.
The beast sprang out!
It was a horrible sight.
The beast had the head of a lion,
the body of a goat,
and the tail of a snake.
Flames burst from
its mouth.

Pegasus beat his wings.
He flew away from the flames.
The prince shot arrow
after arrow.

But the arrows did not hurt
the beast!

24

The prince did not know
what to do.

"Help me, Athena!" he cried.
And then he heard a voice.

"Remember your dream,"
Athena said.

"I sent Pegasus to you.
I sent you a spear.
They both are magic.
Use them to kill the beast."

So the prince raised
his mighty spear.
He and Pegasus flew
toward the beast.

The green smoke was so thick.

The flames were so hot.

But the prince did not stop.

He thrust the magic spear

right at the beast.

The beast let out a roar—

and fell to the ground.

Dead!

After the battle,
the prince and Pegasus
flew home.
The prince was a hero!

What did Pegasus do?

He took to the sky.

He flew back to the gods.

Many years later,

Pegasus died.

The gods honored him.

They made a picture

of Pegasus.

The picture was made of stars.
You can still see Pegasus
on a clear night.
The magic white horse
is still flying high.